MY BABYSITTER IS A ROBOT

ILLUSTRATED BY
DAVE COUSINS CATALINA ECHEVERRI

stripes

CHAPTER 1

LIKE GRANDMA
(WITH A BEARD)

"A ROBOT!"

I grinned. "Cool, huh?"

"I can't believe you've got a ROBOT for a babysitter!" Ali shook his head. "That is so not fair! I have to go home *with my auntie* and look after my little cousins while you get to hang out with A ROBOT!"

"Ask if you can come round to mine then."

My best friend pulled a face. "*No fun until all your homework is done!*" he said in his *auntie* voice. Ali's great at voices – he cracks me up

1

every time. "Hey, what do you think it'll look like?" he said, reaching for his coat. "Maybe your robot will be all gold like C-3PO from *Star Wars*. Or a Transformer like Optimus Prime – or Bumblebee! How cool would THAT be?"

"Grandma said she was making a robot that looked like a human, so people wouldn't be able to tell what it was."

"Oh, yeah! I forgot your grandma made it." Ali looked worried. He was probably thinking about the **AUTOMATIC PORRIDGE MACHINE**. I still had nightmares about that, and Ali hadn't been allowed to sleep over at mine since.

I should probably explain. My grandma is an inventor. She makes all kinds of gadgets and machines. Some of them even work … sort of.

"Hey," said Ali, lowering his voice. "Do you think if Brett knows you've got a killer robot, he might leave us alone?" We glanced across the cloakroom to where Brett Burton was emptying the contents of someone's bag on to the floor.

"I dunno. I think Grandma probably programmed it to be a babysitter, not a killing machine."

For a moment Ali looked disappointed, then his face lit up. "Hi, Ivana!"

I didn't get why Ali thought Ivana was so great. She was best friends with my twin sister for a start, which showed a severe lack of judgement if you ask me!

"Hi, Jess," said Ali, with less enthusiasm.

My sister didn't answer, just steered Ivana towards the door as though we didn't exist.

Ali was so busy smiling at Ivana that he didn't see Brett coming. The shove sent us both flying. I tripped over my bag and Ali landed on top of me.

"Watch where you're going!" said Brett, snorting as he lurched off in search of his next victim.

"I don't care what your grandma designed that robot for," said Ali, helping me up. "I'm still going to ask it if it can sort Brett out!"

When I saw my sister waiting at the edge
of the playground, I knew straight away that
something was wrong.

Jess is my twin, which means we've been
stuck with each other our entire lives. I can't
even have a birthday without her getting in
the way! Of course Jess behaves like it's all MY
fault, as if I got born *deliberately* just to spoil
her fun. When we're at school, we try to have
as little to do with each other as possible,
which can be difficult when you're stuck in the
same class. So I can promise you that my sister
does NOT wait to walk home with me.

"Don't go out there!" Jess dragged me and
Ali back against the wall. "It's at the gate!" she
said. "WAITING FOR US!"

It took me a few seconds to work out that
she was talking about the robot. Jess was less

excited by the idea than me.

I peeked round the corner and spotted our new babysitter straight away. I'd like to say it was because our dog Digby was standing beside it, but that would be a lie. The robot was simply impossible to miss.

"Oh!" said Ali.

I wasn't sure *Oh!* quite covered it…

The thing is, as well as being an inventor, Grandma is a great believer in RECYCLING. She has three sheds, a garage and two bedrooms in her house full of stuff that "only needs a ___" (fill in the blank). Like the bicycle that "only needs a *wheel*", and the giant grandfather clock that "only needs an *hour hand*". It tells perfect time and chimes obediently every hour, except you can never be sure *which* hour.

6

The list goes on, but I won't. You get the idea.

Grandma hates waste, so the things she invents are always made from bits of other things that weren't meant to go together. Which probably explained why our new babysitter was wearing Grandma's old coat – the red one with the pink flowers and the furry collar.

"It looks like Father Christmas!" Jess groaned. "Look at that BEARD!"

"Grandma says that the beard hides the joins so you can't see it's not a real person!" I told her.

"Well, duh!" She frowned. "Hey! Are those my old Barbie skates?"

"And Dad's football hat."

"Um, I should get going," said Ali. "Auntie's waiting." He was embarrassed for me. We'd been expecting a cool robot like Bumblebee

… but the thing waiting at the gates looked more like Grandma with a beard!

I watched my friend run across the playground to where his aunt and a gaggle of little cousins were waiting. I was beginning to think that *he* was the lucky one.

Grandma must have programmed the robot to recognize us because as soon as we emerged from our hiding place it started waving.

"Miss Jess," said the robot. "Master Jake! How lovely to meet you." It sounded like Grandma putting on a deep voice, which is exactly what it was.

Grandma recorded the voices for all her inventions herself. If the robot was male, like this one, she used the computer to make her voice deeper, but it still sounded like Grandma doing a funny voice.

"My name's Jake," I told him. "JUST Jake!"

"My apologies, Master Just Jake," said the robot.

"NO! I didn't mean—"

Jess snorted. "So what's *your* name?"

"My name is Robin," said the robot. "Very pleased to make your acquaintance."

"Where's the car?" I asked, anxious to get away from school before too many people saw us with this bearded, roller-skating excuse for a robot.

"There are lots of cars. Which one would you like me to locate, Master Just Jake?"

"OUR car! The one we need to go home in!"

The robot tilted his head to one side

and stroked his beard. Grandma must have programmed him to do that while he was processing information – a bit like the spinning wheel you get on the computer when you're waiting for files to open.

Finally he spoke. "Today's method of transportation to … HOME … will be … WALKING."

"WHAT? You're joking! Do you know how FAR that is?"

"Zero point four six miles," said the robot. "At average walking speed we should reach our destination in seven point three minutes."

I groaned with frustration. "Why didn't you bring the car? Please tell me Grandma programmed you to drive."

"As you wish." The robot paused and cleared his throat. "Master Just Jake, it gives me great pleasure to inform you that your grandma programmed me with the ability to drive."

Jess collapsed into a fit of giggles.

"I can also ride a bicycle, fly a plane and operate the missile-launch facility on a nuclear submarine."

My sister stopped laughing and gaped at the robot.

"If you can do all those things, why are we WALKING?" I was so angry, my voice came out in an embarrassing squeak.

"Walking is an ideal form of daily exercise," said the robot, sounding like he was reading from a website (which he probably was).

I noticed that when Robin needed to say certain words – ones Grandma hadn't expected – he used the same electronic voice as the computer at home. So you'd have the deep grandma voice, then a word or two in an electro voice. It all just added to the strangeness.

"A relaxed stroll strengthens bones and muscles," said the robot. "It reduces the risk of heart disease and helps you lose weight. Walking also increases the supply of oxygen to the brain which can make you more intelligent!"

"Pity it's only zero point four six miles," said Jess. "Maybe you should walk round the block a few times, Jake."

"Ha ha! You're not…" I stopped.

Jess turned to see what I was looking at and groaned.

Just when I thought the day couldn't get any worse…

FAKES, SKATES
AND DROOL

It was too late to cross the road. From the grin on Brett's face I knew he'd seen us. Most of the time THE BANE OF MY LIFE lurches around like a zombie, but when he senses an opportunity to ruin someone's day Brett's face lights up like a pumpkin at Halloween.

Jess was more worried about the girl he was with. While Brett was into simple, physical acts of torture – dead legs and flicking bogeys into your hair – stuff that didn't use up too much of his limited brainpower, his cousin Olivia was pure EVIL. She *looked* totally harmless, friendly even. Olivia was always the first to put up her hand in class, but it was all an act. If Olivia decided she didn't like you, she and her gang of Little Olivia Clones would make your life hell.

Jess and Olivia had actually been friends when they were younger (and didn't know any better!). Then in Year Three an argument over a copy of *Charlie and the Chocolate Factory* turned into a full-on brawl. They've been sworn enemies ever since.

Dribbling along behind them was Olivia's little brother Drool (real name Dayton). Unlike his immaculate sister, Drool usually looks like he's just climbed out of a dustbin. He also suffers from a severe case of *leakage* (hence the nickname). Drool is bad for Olivia's image, so being with him always puts her in a worse mood than usual. Lucky us.

They stopped and fanned out across the pavement, blocking our escape.

Olivia's eyes swept across us and settled
on the robot. "Nice skates," she said.

"Thank you," said Robin, totally missing
the fact that she was being sarcastic.

"They go really well with your coat,"
said Olivia, making Brett snigger. "You *must*
tell me where you got that. I simply *have*

to get one!"

"Here! Have mine," said Robin, reaching for the buttons.

"NO!" Jess pulled his hands away.

I guessed she was thinking the same as me: whatever the robot had on under that coat, we did *not* want it displayed in public! Knowing Grandma and her weird sense of humour, she'd probably given Robin some kind of underwear – quite possibly her own! THAT did not bear thinking about.

"She doesn't really want your coat," I told Robin. "She's just taking the mickey."

The robot did his *strokey-beard-thinking-thing* again. "Oh! I didn't know I had a *mickey* to give her."

Olivia rolled her eyes. "Was that supposed to be a joke?" She peered at Robin. "Who IS this anyway? Your grandad?"

"Oh, no, I'm not their grandfather! I'm—"

"He's a friend of our grandma!" said Jess quickly. "Just visiting."

Olivia scowled.

"I like your footwear also," said Robin, pointing to her trainers.

Grandma must have programmed the robot to be polite, but without realizing it Robin had made a clever move. The one thing Olivia likes more than being horrible to people is talking about how great she is.

"I know," she said, her face breaking into a smile. "I can't even TELL you how much they cost! My dad got them from America. You can't buy them over here." She lifted a foot to give us a better view of the trainers. "Designed by Carly-G herself. That's her ACTUAL signature on the side there."

"Mmm," said Robin, peering at the trainer. "That's actually a printed reproduction."

"WHAT DID YOU SAY?" Olivia's foot slammed back on to the pavement.

"The signature on the side of your sports shoe," said Robin, smiling. "It's printed. If you look closely, you can see it's made up of tiny dots of ink."

I held my breath, waiting for Olivia to ask how Robin could possibly see a detail like that – oh, unless he was a robot with mega-zoom eyesight of course!

But Olivia was too shocked to speak.

"Carly-G only signed a hundred special-edition pairs herself," said Robin. "The ones you are wearing are reproduction copies made in China."

Olivia's face had a gone a strange colour. Her mouth was moving, but no words were coming out.

"You mean they're FAKES!" said Brett, finally catching up with what was happening.

"NO!" squeaked Olivia, finding her voice again. "These are REAL! Special! Limited edition! They were signed PERSONALLY by Carly-G!" She sounded like she was trying to convince herself as much as us.

For a few seconds it almost felt like a victory! I should have known better.

Olivia turned to Robin. "How would YOU know anything about it anyway? I bet you don't even know who Carly-G is!"

"Carly-G is a singer and actress," said the robot, in his reading-from-the-internet voice. "Her first acting job was on the Disney Channel, aged seven. She is best known—"

"Robin's a big fan!" said Jess, giving a nervous laugh. "He and Grandma are always playing Carly-G and dancing round the kitchen. *Sooo* embarrassing!"

For a moment Olivia looked totally

confused, then she leaned in close and hissed into my sister's face. "You tell anyone about this and you're DEAD!"

Just then a large black car pulled in to the kerb, and suddenly Olivia was all smiles.

"Here's Grandad!" she said, dragging Drool out from under the hedge.

The three of them piled into the back seat as the driver's window slid down. A large pointy nose emerged and seemed to sniff the air, while a pair of black eyes gazed suspiciously at us.

"Hello, Mr Burton," said Jess.

As well as being Olivia, Brett and Drool's grandad, Mr Burton was our next-door neighbour.

The old man smiled without showing his teeth. "I don't think we've met," he said, peering at our new babysitter.

"My name's Robin." The robot held out his hand. "Very pleased to make your acquaintance."

Mr Burton reluctantly reached out to shake hands, but the moment he touched Robin's glove, our neighbour's face changed. His eyes widened, then filled with a hungry excitement that sent a chill right through me.

"How interesting," he said. Then the window slid back up and the car drove away.

"What did you do that for?" said Jess, glaring at the robot.

"I believe it is the custom to shake hands on first meeting someone."

"Not THAT! Why did you tell Olivia that her trainers were fakes?"

"Because they are." Robin sounded puzzled.

"That's not the point! You don't tell OLIVIA that her clothes are rubbish!"

The robot clutched at his beard, clearly confused. "I didn't mean to cause offence. I was trying to be helpful."

"You've just made things **A HUNDRED TIMES WORSE!**" Jess was really shouting now. "If Brett tells anyone at school that Olivia's trainers are fakes – which he will – she'll blame it on me!" My sister turned and stormed off down the road. I could tell she was trying not to cry.

"How did you know anyway?" I asked the robot. "About the trainers?"

"I looked them up on the internet," he said. "I have constant online access from within my central processing unit."

"You mean your brain's got built-in Wi-Fi? Wow!" Maybe this robot wasn't so lame after all. "The look on Olivia's face when you said her trainers were fake… That was classic!"

"The girl said she liked my coat," the robot explained. "I was making polite conversation – sometimes known as 'chit-chat' or 'having a natter'."

"She was being sarcastic," I told him. "It's when someone says something that sounds like they're being nice, but actually they're making fun of you."

"How confusing."

"It's a human thing," I said. "Don't worry

about it."

The robot nodded. "Thank you, Master Just Jake. I will add that information to my database."

I nodded, but I couldn't help wondering what other important knowledge might be missing from Robin's brain.

CHAPTER 3

A RULE-OBSESSED FUN SPONGE

Mr Burton was in his front garden with a leaf-blower when we got home. This struck me as odd because there weren't any leaves on the ground. His eyes followed us all the way to the front door.

The moment we got inside, I dumped my bag and headed for the stairs. I'd arranged to meet up online with Ali later, to play *Revenge of the Robots*. We'd been trying to get through the last level of the game for over a week, but the boss robot was too powerful and we kept getting killed. I wanted to get some practice in.

"One moment, Master Just Jake," said Robin. "My instructions state that all homework must be completed before recreational activities are allowed."

"That's OK, I don't have any homework tonight," I lied.

But the robot was already stroking his beard. "Accessing homework online," he said in his computer voice. *Class Z: Design a poster for the school fair. Due in tomorrow."* Robin came out of his trance and his beard twitched into a smile. "I'll get the felt tips out, shall I?"

I stomped back down the stairs. Maybe a babysitter with instant online access wasn't so cool after all.

Robin made me and Jess sit at the table –
TOGETHER – to do our homework. It took
us hours to make posters that he was happy
with. Every time one of us told the robot
we'd finished, he'd spot some important piece
of information we'd forgotten, or point out
that we'd spelled something wrong. Then he
made us colour them in, standing over us like
a prison guard. It was dark outside by the time
he let me go upstairs.

It felt like barely five minutes later when
Robin knocked on my bedroom door. "Your
thirty minutes of game time are almost up,
Master Just Jake!" he said, walking in.

"What? It can't be!"

"You have exactly fifty-three seconds left,"
said the robot.

"Yeah, OK! I just need to get to the end of
this level." I didn't dare take my eyes off the
screen. Me and Ali were being pinned down

by a swarm of seriously scary, giant robotic insects. It was the furthest we'd got through the level.

"Ten seconds, Master Just Jake," said Robin.

"Yeah, I just need to finish this."

"Five seconds."

I was low on health and ammo.

"Four."

I had to make the last few attacks count.

"Three."

"Do you have to count?"

"Two."

"You're really not helping!"

"One."

The screen went black.

"WHAT? NO!" I shook the controller, staring at the dead console in disbelief.

"Your thirty minutes are up, Master Just Jake."

I looked at the robot. **"YOU SWITCHED IT OFF?"**

"Your mother's instructions were very clear," he said. "Thirty minutes' game time only."

"You don't just pull the plug IN THE MIDDLE OF A GAME! Mum would've let me finish the level! When she says thirty minutes, she doesn't mean EXACTLY – to the SECOND!"

Jess appeared in the doorway to see what all the shouting was about.

"HE PULLED THE PLUG ON ME!" I still couldn't quite believe it.

Just then the doorbell rang and Robin went downstairs to answer it.

"At least you got to play," said Jess. "He just made me practise the recorder – for FIFTEEN WHOLE MINUTES!"

"I wondered what that noise was," I said. "I thought it was the screams of dying robots in my game."

Jess stuck out her tongue. "It's NOT FUNNY!"

For once I had to agree with her. "I thought a robot babysitter would be so cool – but no! Grandma has to invent some rule-obsessed fun sponge who looks like Father Christmas gone wrong!"

I could hear Robin downstairs talking to Mr Burton. It must have been him at the door. I wondered what he wanted.

"We need to do something," said Jess, "before this gets out of hand."

"Have you got a plan?"

"I'm working on it."

There was a look in my sister's eyes as she said it that almost made me feel sorry for the robot.

But Jess didn't come up with anything.

And things just got worse.

FOUL PLAY

"Your sister *reeeeally* doesn't like that number seven," said Ali.

The referee showed Jess a yellow card, then helped the opposing striker back to his feet.

It was Friday after school. An icy wind cut across the field as me, Ali and Ivana shivered on the touchline. Our Year Six football team was playing a school from across town. The game was barely ten minutes old, but Jess had already delivered three bone-crunching tackles. Pretty impressive when you consider she plays in goal!

"Go and get warmed up, Ali," said Mrs Badoe, waddling down the touchline towards us. "We'll have to take Jess off if she carries on like this."

"But I'm rubbish in goal!" said Ali, doing a few half-hearted stretches.

"At least you won't get yourself sent off." Our teacher frowned and rubbed the bump protruding from her coat.

"How's the baby, miss?" said Ivana.

"She's kicking just like Jess today!" said Mrs Badoe, chuckling as she walked back down the touchline.

"Jess is in a bad mood because of that

robot," said Ivana, pointing across the pitch to where Robin and Digby were watching the game with Mr Burton.

I nodded. By breaktime the day after THE INCIDENT, word had spread that the Carly-G trainers Olivia had been bragging about were fake. Olivia probably knew it was Brett who had spilled her secret, but she still took it out on Jess.

"Why's your robot standing with Brett's grandad?" said Ali.

"I don't know." I'd been wondering why Mr Burton was even here – neither Brett nor Olivia played football.

The old man had been sniffing around Robin ever since that first day after school. Just that morning I'd caught him spying on us through binoculars from an upstairs window. I wondered if he'd realized that Robin was actually a robot.

As I watched, Robin waved his wooden rattle and shouted words of encouragement to the team.

Of course, rather than yelling "good pass" or "nice shot" – like a normal person – the robot was urging Northfield Park Year Sixes on with phrases such as, "Play up, chaps! Their backs are wilting!"

It was like he'd looked up a list of 'Things to shout at a football match' – from the 1900s!

"Is he like this all the time?" Ivana asked.

I nodded. "We had to go for a haircut after school on Wednesday, and he tried to get Mr Rossini to give Digby a shave! I swear he thinks that dog is our REALLY HAIRY little brother!"

"I thought robots were supposed to be clever," said Ali.

"Yeah! Trust us to get the world's first stupid one!" I shook my head. "I reckon Grandma programmed him in a hurry and forgot to include some important bits of information – like the small fact that Digby IS A DOG!"

Ivana giggled.

"I wish I could see the funny side," I said. "We almost got done for shoplifting last night!"

Ali stopped his warm-up and stared at me. "What happened?"

"You know that sign above the baskets in the corner shop? Where it says *PLEASE TAKE ONE*?"

Ali nodded.

"Well, he did! Our dopey robot thought it was a free basket to carry your shopping home in! The guy in the shop chased us down the road IN FRONT OF EVERYONE!"

"I suppose that *is* what it means literally," said Ali.

"The trouble is he takes EVERYTHING literally! He's got no common sense!"

"That's robots for you," said Ali.

"Yeah, and I've had enough. Films make robots look really cool, but in real life they're just a pain!"

"You should tell your parents," said Ivana.

I snorted. "Dad's always away driving his lorry. I tried talking to Mum, but she just went on about how if she didn't have to do three jobs we wouldn't need a babysitter. But she does, so we do, and we can't really afford to pay anyone. That's why Grandma offered to make us a robot babysitter."

"If you think about it," said Ali slowly, "a robot's just a computer on legs."

"So?"

"So … computers are always going wrong, aren't they? My brother's laptop stopped working when he spilled a can of Coke on it."

I looked at him. "So you think that if we spilled some Coke on Robin – accidentally on purpose – he might stop working?"

Ali nodded. "He'll be all like…" My friend started making choking sounds, twitching his shoulders and waving his arms around.

"STOP IT!" said Ivana. "That's horrible!"

Ali stopped.

Ivana was right. I didn't want to actually harm the robot, just make Mum send him back to Grandma. Before I could think any more about it, there was an audible crunch from the pitch, followed by a howl and the sound of the referee's whistle.

"Uh-oh!" said Ali. "Looks like I might be going in goal after all!"

"Mrs Badoe said I'm not allowed to play for the next two matches!" Jess flung her football boots across the kitchen. Digby ran after them, thinking it was a game.

"AND she might choose Liesha for the penalty shoot-out stall at the fair now!"

"Just because you got sent off?"

Jess nodded. "It's all HIS fault." She scowled at Robin, who was trying to wrestle her boots back from the dog.

"I'll put these by the back door, Miss Jess," said the robot, dragging Digby across the floor, still attached to the boots. "You can clean them when we've finished making the cakes."

"Cakes?" I said. "What cakes?"

"To take to Olivia's party," growled Jess.

"That's TOMORROW?!"

Olivia was having a pool party and picnic at the local sports centre. She'd invited the whole class.

"Do we have to go?" The thought of being anywhere near deep water when Brett was around seemed like a really bad idea. "Olivia only invited everyone so she can show off and get more presents!"

"You think I haven't begged Mum not to make us go?" said Jess. "You know what she's like. Just cos *she's* friends with Olivia's mum, she thinks me and Olivia must still be friends too!"

"But why do we have to make cakes?"

"Because we could only afford a small present, Mum thinks it'd be nice to take cakes for everyone." Jess shook her head. "I told her there was NO WAY I'm making cakes for

HER, with HIM!"

"What did she say?"

My sister's brow scrunched into a concertina of rage. "She wasn't even listening! She just told me we might need the new packet of sugar in the cupboard…"

Jess stopped suddenly, and the frown fell from her face.

"Oh!" she said. "Now there's an idea…"

"What?"

"I think I might have found a way to get rid of that robot!" she said.

RUBBING SALT IN THE WOUND

"You're putting SALT in the SUGAR jar! THAT'S your great plan?"

Jess sighed and rolled her eyes. "Think about it. We get the robot to *help us* make some cakes for Olivia's party, except he uses salt instead of sugar. They'll be DISGUSTING! One of Olivia's princessy friends might even be SICK!"

It was the happiest I'd seen my sister all week.

"There'll definitely be complaints. We just

need to make sure Mum knows it was Robin who made the cakes. If it looks like he nearly poisoned half the class, she'll send him back to Grandma for sure!"

I felt a smile spread slowly across my lips. "This isn't easy for me to admit," I told her, "but sometimes, sis … you're a genius! In a scary, really evil, taking-over-the-world kind of way."

Robin put on Dad's apron to bake the cakes. He was still wearing Grandma's coat underneath, skating round the kitchen like Father Christmas on ice! I noticed he was making a strange noise while he worked.

"Is that … singing?"

"My database informs me that people often sing while completing a task that makes them happy," said Robin. "I am enjoying baking

43

with you, so I thought it would be appropriate to express my happiness through the medium of song."

"Please don't," said Jess. "It's really annoying."

The robot apologized, and I felt a bit sorry for him.

Making the cakes wasn't actually as bad as I expected. Robin had the recipe in his head, so me and Jess just weighed out ingredients while the robot stirred them all together in a big bowl. Before he started, Robin unscrewed one of his hands and replaced it with an attachment like you get on a food mixer. Watching him remove his own hand was kind of gross but also strangely cool. The best part was we didn't have to get arm ache trying to stir the mixture. The robot just put his new mixer hand in the bowl and *whirrrrrrrrrr!* – off it went! It was kind of impressive.

I realized I was actually quite enjoying myself – not that I was about to start singing or anything outrageous like that, but it was a good laugh baking with Robin. When he offered to let us taste the mixture, I almost said *yes*, until I remembered we'd used SALT instead of SUGAR. It was kind of disappointing because I reckon if we'd used the right ingredients, Robin's cakes would have been amazing.

Mum came home just as we were taking the cakes out of the oven.

"I popped in to change before I start my shift at the pub," she said, dumping her bag on the kitchen table. "Those cakes smell amazing!"

"It was ALL Robin," said Jess. "He did ALL the work so he should take ALL the credit!"

"Oh, that's very kind of you, Miss Jess, but I'd say it was a team effort." The robot slid the freshly baked muffins on to a cooling rack. "Would you like to try one, ma'am?"

"I shouldn't really," said Mum, drooling already. "They're for Olivia's party. But they do smell delicious. Maybe I should sample one – just to make sure they're OK?"

An evil gleam flickered in my sister's eyes.

"Anyone else?" said Mum, reaching for a muffin.

"Maybe later," said Jess.

"I'm not really in a cake mood," I lied.

Mum took a bite. I stepped back out of range. If Jess was right, that mouthful would come flying back out at any moment.

I watched Mum's face, waiting for a cough, a cry of horror, as she tasted salt where there should have been sugar.

"Mmmmm!" said Mum, closing her eyes. "This is AMAZING! Robin, you're a genius!"

Me and Jess exchanged a puzzled look.

"I'm very glad you like it," said Robin.
"However, I was wondering – would you like
me to do an inventory of your ingredients?"

Mum frowned.

"While we were baking, I noticed the jar
marked *SUGAR* actually contained SALT!"
said Robin. "My sensors detected the mistake

before any damage was done, but I'd be happy to run a diagnostic check on all your food-storage units." He smiled but his eyes swung round towards me and Jess as he said it – like he knew what we'd tried to do!

"That must have been me!" said Mum. "I've been so tired lately. Thank goodness you were here to spot it, Robin!"

Yeah, lucky us!

"That went well," I muttered as Mum headed for the door. "Now Mum thinks she's found her very own *Bake Off* champion, it's going to be even harder to get rid of him."

"Oh, shut up!" said Jess and stomped off upstairs.

UNEXPECTED OBJECT
IN THE WATER

GAME OVER!

The words filled the screen in large red letters then crumbled into flickering pixels.

I threw down the controller in disgust. It was pointless – this robot was impossible to defeat.

"Dead again, huh?"

I gave an involuntary yelp of surprise, then turned to glare at my sister. "You're supposed to KNOCK! Not just barge into my room!"

"I did knock. Twice. You couldn't hear

because you were too busy shouting at Ali and squealing like a baby."

"I don't squeal!"

Jess raised an eyebrow.

"What do you WANT anyway?"

"It's time for Olivia's party."

"I can't go, I'm ill!"

"No, you're not. Anyway I already tried that. Turns out Grandma's annoying robot can do full medical diagnostic scans." My sister waved a sheet of paper at me. "This says I'm low on iron and need to eat more greens."

"That's it then," I said. "We're doomed!"

At least we didn't have to walk to the swimming pool. No, this time we took the bus! Luckily there was nobody onboard we knew. I still kept my hood up all the way though, just in case.

It was weird. Usually I try to have as little to do with my sister as possible, but since Robin's arrival our on-going feud had been put on hold. We both realized that the only chance we had of getting rid of the robot was to join forces and work together.

Which was why I found myself sitting at the back of the bus next to my sister, while the robot and Digby shared a seat near the front. Digby was perched on the robot's lap, happily watching as Robin pointed out things through the window and chatted to him, as though the dog could actually understand what he was saying.

"Maybe we could lose him at the swimming pool..." said Jess. "Maybe Robin could *accidentally* fall in? I bet water wouldn't be good for his circuits."

I pictured Ali doing his jerky dance. "Isn't that a bit mean?"

Jess came closer to give me the full benefit of her glare. "That *thing* is ruining our lives! We *need* to get rid of it!"

I still felt bad about hurting the robot, but things *were* getting desperate. I imagined Robin picking us up every day from school; more embarrassing trips to the barber's and the shops; the fact that he would always know what homework we had and if we were faking an illness; not to mention the trouble he'd got us into with Olivia…

Much as I hated to admit it, I knew my sister was right.

It was Saturday so the sports centre was busy. I kept my head down and my hood up as we followed the robot inside. He had Digby tucked under his arm as he led the way into the changing rooms, his skates skidding and sliding on the tiled floor.

I dived into the nearest cubicle, thinking if I could get changed and into the pool quickly, nobody would need to know that Robin was anything to do with me. Then I realized I didn't have the bag with my trunks in.

I could hear Jess moving around in the cubicle next door.

"Hey! Have you got the bag with the stuff in?"

"I've got MY bag with MY things. You gave yours to Robin to carry."

I cursed my laziness. Now I was going to have to find him. Unfortunately locating the robot was all too easy. I simply followed the sound of laughter drifting from the pool.

The noise grew louder as I approached. I could see Olivia's parents and Mr Burton in the spectator seats, and Ali with some of the other kids from my class already in the water. They were all staring and pointing at something. I took a deep breath and stepped out.

The robot was by the steps at the shallow
end — he couldn't have looked more out
of place in his coat, hat and skates! But that
wasn't why people were gawking.

Digby stood shivering at the water's edge,
his hairy back legs poking out from the
bottom of my blue swim shorts
with the sharks on. The
dog's tail poked up through
the waistband at the top
and it wasn't wagging.
Robin was blowing air
into a bright orange water wing. The other one
was already in place round Digby's front leg.

"WHAT ARE YOU DOING?"
I shouted, forgetting I was supposed to be
keeping a low profile.

"Ah, there you are, Master Just Jake!"
Robin's beard quivered as he smiled. "I'm
getting the little one ready for swimming."

56

"But he's a DOG! And those are MY trunks!"

The robot's eyebrows shot upwards in surprise. He looked down at Digby as though seeing him for the first time. "A dog!" he said. "How interesting. I will update my database accordingly."

Suddenly I was aware that the swimming pool had gone very quiet. I could feel a million pairs of eyes staring at us. Of course the Birthday Girl was loving my moment of public humiliation. I doubt Olivia would have looked more delighted if Carly-G herself had arrived at that moment to personally sign a pair of trainers for her!

"Jake?" I turned round. Jess and Ivana were standing behind me.

My sister's eyes widened as she took in the scene. "Why's Digby wearing your swimming trunks?"

Which was when the laughter started up again.

Dogs *know* when they're being laughed at. Digby hates it. He gets embarrassed. And when Digby gets embarrassed, his first instinct is to run and hide. Sure enough, the dog shot off round the pool, still wearing my trunks and the single water wing.

"Don't worry, Master Just Jake," said the robot. "I'll get him!"

The thing is, roller-skates aren't designed for use on slippery tiles, and the moment Robin tried to follow Digby his skates went in two different directions.

He skidded…

Slipped…

Spun round a couple of times … then started skating BACKWARDS towards the deep end, flapping his arms like he was trying to take off.

58

I could hear Robin apologizing as people screamed and dived into the water to get out of the way.

"I'm terribly sorry!"

"Do excuse me!"

"Marvellous dive, by the way – exquisite technique!"

Digby was also in trouble. As he ran, my trunks slipped and wrapped themselves round his legs. The dog tried to stop, but he couldn't grip the tiled floor and shot towards the water like a hairy torpedo.

If Robin hadn't skated past and grabbed him, the dog would have ended up in the pool. And with my trunks binding his legs together Digby wouldn't have been able to swim.

For a moment it looked like the robot had saved the day, until I realized that he too was unable to stop. I suddenly saw that there was only one way this was going to end.

The diving pit was next to the main pool. With a low springboard for training purposes.

"Oh, no…" said Jess.

The robot shot on to the board and sprang into the air. He did a perfect somersault … then the BEST WATER BOMB I'VE EVER SEEN!

The splash almost emptied the pool of water. It created a tidal wave that swept over the balcony, nearly drowning a dozen pensioners who had gathered for a scone-eating contest in the café.

First there was an open-mouthed, jaw-dropped silence. Then Ali started to applaud.

Soon everyone at the pool (except the soggy pensioners) was clapping and cheering as Robin and Digby were dragged, dripping, from the water by Mr Burton and the lifeguards. Even some of Olivia's friends joined in until she silenced them with a glare.

"That was incredible," said Ivana. "He's so brave to rescue the dog!"

I was stunned.

"What's happening?" said Jess.

"I'm not sure," I said. "But it looks like everyone thinks Robin is actually ... kind of cool."

"But ... he went into the water," said Jess. "How is he still working?"

I couldn't answer that, but I realized I was glad the robot was OK. Which didn't make any sense at all. But then it was turning out to be that sort of a day.

CHAPTER 7

THE SECOND WAVE

Mechanical laughter boomed round the room as the robot loomed over me, its red eyes burning like lasers. This was it – the end. I knew I shouldn't have tried to attack it… All I'd done was make the robot angry.

"Now!" said Robin. "Hold down *L2*, press *X* and roll!"

"But that—"

The robot reared up and raised its razor-sharp pincers.

"Master, I highly recommend that you do as

I suggest quite soon – preferably before that rather large mechanical spider bites your head off!"

I frantically stabbed the controls as instructed, then watched as my on-screen avatar ducked and rolled between the giant robot's legs and out the other side.

"Now turn and aim at its weak spot," said Robin.

This time I followed his advice without hesitation.

The massive metal spider howled with rage as my arrows pierced its soft underbelly. Its lethal steel pincers snapped at the air for a few seconds, then its body exploded into a trillion pieces of molten metal.

Finally the screen flashed up the message I'd been waiting weeks to see:

LEVEL COMPLETE.
THE ROBOTS ARE DEFEATED!

"Yes!" I jumped up from my bed and punched the air.

On-screen, Ali's avatar joined me in a victory dance.

"Congratulations, Master Just Jake," said Robin, his voice bubbling slightly as though he was talking underwater.

"We couldn't have done it without your help!"

Robin had spent the last HOUR guiding me and Ali through the final level of *Revenge of the Robots*.

"Those mechanical insects were very badly behaved," he said.

"It made me rather ashamed to be a robot!"

"You're different," I told him. "You're nothing like the robots in the game."

"Thank you, Master Just Jake!" Robin did that twitchy-beard smile of his. "If I can be of no more service, I should go and check on Miss Jess."

When he stood up, a trickle of water ran down from the robot's ear. Robin had leaked all the way home from the party, but other than that he seemed none the worse for his accidental swim.

It was me and Jess who felt different. When we'd got back from the sports centre, we'd expected Robin to start dishing out chores or insisting we did some *fun yet educational* activity with him. Instead he'd said we could do whatever we wanted. We liked this 'new' relaxed version of Robin.

It should have been a clue, a warning – but we ignored it.

"NOOOOOOO!"

At first I thought the scream was part of my game, then I realized it had come from outside.

The second cry — *"JAAAKE!"* — confirmed it.

Jess and Robin were playing football in the garden. Having been banned for two matches, my sister was desperate for any chance to play, even if it was only a kick-about.

Normally I would have ignored her, but there was something in that shriek that made me think I should at least check.

When I opened the back door, Digby shot past me into the house like he'd been fired from a cannon. For some reason he was dripping wet. It took a few seconds for my eyes to make sense of what I was seeing.

Dad's greenhouse was missing half its glass and the tomato plants inside looked like they'd exploded. I could see my sister's football lying in the middle of the mess, so it didn't take a genius to work out what had happened.

But that didn't explain why Robin and Jess appeared to be playing tug-of-war with the hosepipe. I ducked as a snake of high-pressure water swept over my head and drummed against the kitchen window.

"HELP ME!" shouted Jess. "He's gone crazy!"

I ran towards her, but my sister screamed at me to **"TURN OFF THE TAP!"**

"Oh, yeah! Good idea!"

Robin got very upset when the water stopped. He started going on about how the tomatoes needed watering. His voice was all jerky, and he kept repeating the same words over and over.

"What's wrong with him?!" I said. "What did you do?"

"ME? Nothing! One minute he was fine – then he just booted the football into the greenhouse!" My sister wiped strands of wet hair away from her face. "He said the plants needed watering and turned on the hose! But then he started to water Mum's PAINTINGS of Dad's tomatoes, rather than THE ACTUAL TOMATOES themselves!"

"Mum's PAINTINGS!"

Our mum spent her days cleaning offices,

answering phones and serving drinks in a pub, but in her heart she was an artist. When Mum wasn't working, she spent as much time as she could in her shed at the bottom of the garden, painting.

In all the excitement I hadn't noticed that the door to Mum's shed was open. A newly formed river was flowing out across the lawn, with Mum's pictures floating on the surface like brightly decorated rafts.

The robot was pointing at them. "Tomatoes need a regular – regular supply of water – water," he said in his soggy, stuttering voice. "Irregular supply – will cause – cause problems. Water problems. Must water – the tomatoes. Tomatoes. Water. Water, everywhere, but not a drop to drink…"

"Water must have got into his circuits when he fell in the swimming pool!" I said.

"Duh!" said Jess, fighting to keep Robin away from the tap. "But what are we going to DO about it, genius? What if he decides the rest of the house needs watering, too? I don't know how much longer I can hold him!"

FROM BAD...
TO WORSE

Grandma picked up on the second ring. "Hello?"

"Hi, Grandma, it's Jake."

"Oh, hello, Jake. I'm in Milton Keynes. They have concrete cows! Did you know that?"

"Um, no, but … the thing is … your robot – I think there's something wrong with him."

A loud snort tickled my ear. "User error! You can't blame the robot. They're only as good as the person who programmed them."

"That would be you then, Grandma."

"Ah, good point! Which robot are we talking about here?"

"Robin. Our new babysitter."

"Ooh, yes! Good, isn't he? Rather handsome too!"

"Yeah … he's great. I mean, he was, only now he's gone a bit funny. I think he might be malfunctioning."

"Don't be ridiculous! It's probably just teething problems. There are still a few kinks in the software that need ironing out. I'm away at InventorCon at the moment, but when I'm back I'll write you an update patch."

"He's just trashed Dad's greenhouse and watered Mum's paintings."

"Oh," said Grandma. "That sounds like a malfunction to me. What have you done to him?"

"Nothing! Except … there was an incident at the swimming pool this morning…"

"That was you, was it?" said Grandma. "My

friend Eileen called earlier. Furious she was. Said her scone-eating contest got washed away when some clown started showing off in the pool!" She chuckled. "If you got him wet, that *could* have caused a short circuit, which would explain the unexpected behaviour... Have you tried switching him off and on again?"

"How do we do that?"

"You might want to write this down," said Grandma.

"You need to put your finger up his nose."

Jess stared at me. "WHAT?"

"Grandma says there's a reset button up there. You need to 'press and hold for three seconds to initiate a full shutdown'." I checked my notes. "Then we need to give him an hour to dry out before rebooting."

"And this button ... it's UP HIS NOSE?"

"Grandma said she didn't want to put it anywhere it could get nudged accidentally. If you think about it though, it could be worse. She could have hidden it up his—"

"JAKE!"

"I'm just saying – it could be worse."

"Why do I have to do it?"

"You're closest."

Jess glared at me. All the time I'd been on the phone, my sister had been fighting to keep Robin away from the tap, using Digby to herd the robot like a sheepdog. "You'll have to hold him then."

I sneaked up and grabbed the robot from behind, doing my best to pin his arms to his sides. Robin was surprisingly strong – it felt like wrestling an angry vacuum cleaner.

"HURRY UP!"

"Which nostril?" said Jess, her finger poised over the robot's face.

"I don't know! JUST TRY ONE!"

There was a loud squelch. "I think I'm going to be sick," said Jess.

"PRESS AND HOLD FOR THREE SECONDS!" I shouted.

"I'M TRYING!"

Suddenly the robot stopped squirming and went limp in my arms. We both dropped to the ground. When I looked up, my sister was standing over us, staring at her finger. "Ugh – it's covered in robot goo!"

"It's probably just swimming-pool water."

"That's even WORSE!" said Jess.

We dragged Robin to the spare bedroom and got him into bed, then went back downstairs.

"Now we just have to fix this before Mum sees it," said Jess, staring at the remains of our garden.

We'd barely started when Mum burst through the back door.

"Thank goodness you're both OK! I came as soon as I heard."

It took a moment for her words to sink in. "Did Grandma call you?"

"No," said Mum. "Mr Burton saw the whole thing and phoned me at work."

Our neighbour materialized behind Mum like a pantomime baddie (minus the puff of smoke).

"I was about to offer some assistance," he said, "but then I saw you overpower it." His eyes had that greedy gleam in them again, like he was enjoying this.

"I can't thank you enough!" said Mum. "To think I left my children with that murderous thing!"

The old man's face darkened. "That's what happens when people start messing with things they don't understand … building ROBOTS!"

I *knew* he'd worked it out.

"Mr Burton's offered to take Robin away," said Mum.

"WHAT?!"

"That thing needs dismantling before someone gets hurt," said Mr Burton, heading inside with Mum.

"NO! WAIT!" I followed them, and the trail of muddy footprints, up the stairs. "Robin didn't mean any harm. He's just got some water in his circuits. He'll be fine once he's dried out – Grandma said!"

The old man snorted. "Your grandma! I should've guessed *she* was responsible for this!"

I was too busy pleading with Mum to wonder what Mr Burton meant by that.

But Mum had made her decision. "I feel bad enough leaving you with a babysitter as it is," she said. "I never liked the idea of a robot. I shouldn't have let Grandma talk me into it."

There was nothing we could do except watch Mr Burton heave Robin over his shoulder and carry him next door.

"Well, we did *want* to get rid of him," said Jess.

I nodded. She was right. We'd been plotting for days and now we'd got exactly what we wanted.

We should have been celebrating. But for some reason we weren't.

FRACTIONS OF
A WHOLE

"This is Rosalyn," said Mum, "your new babysitter."

"S'up?" The girl almost managed a smile. She had blue hair and a nose ring and looked kind of bored.

"Sorry to dash off," said Mum, "but I'm already late. You all have fun getting to know each other!"

The moment the front door closed, Rosalyn slumped on to the sofa and scowled at us. "Right, listen up. These are the rules. Number one: you don't bother me and I won't bother you."

Me and Jess exchanged a look. Our new babysitter sneezed and pointed at Digby. "Rule number two: keep that dog away from me. I'm allergic!"

I took Digby upstairs to my room. We had a test on Wednesday and Mrs Badoe had given us a whole sheet of stuff to learn. I sat down and stared at it for at least five minutes, but the words just buzzed around like flies and refused to settle anywhere near my brain. Part of the problem was that Ali had lent me a new game. I really wanted to try it out. Maybe once I'd had a go on that, I'd be able to concentrate.

But there was a rule: no gaming until our homework was done. Except Rosalyn had said there were only two rules now and *that* hadn't been on the list!

The disc for *Revenge of the Robots* was still in the console. It made me think about Robin, which brought a weird heavy feeling to my chest.

I shook my head and waited for the new game to load. If Robin was still looking after us, there was no way I'd be allowed to do this. He would have been standing over me, insisting I learn the stuff for the test. This was a much better arrangement. Definitely.

The next day at school, Brett cornered me and Ali in the playground. He looked worryingly alert, which was never a good sign.

"Hey, loser! You know that weird old bloke you were hanging around with? Guess what? IT WAS A ROBOT!"

"Really? Wow! I never knew."

Ali shot me a look of alarm, but Brett was as oblivious to sarcasm as Robin had been.

"My grandad's got it working as his own personal slave," said Brett, his eyes brimming with spiteful glee. "It does all his cooking and cleaning. Even cuts his toenails for him!"

I KNEW IT! All along I'd suspected Mr Burton was up to something. All that rubbish he'd told Mum about dismantling Robin so he wouldn't 'go rogue and wreak havoc' again. It was just a trick to get the robot for himself!

But at least that meant Robin hadn't been destroyed…

I shrugged. "Good luck to him," I said. "That robot was nothing but a pain in the neck." I pushed past Brett and walked away.

Ali had to run to catch up with me. "Imagine having to cut old-man toenails!" he said. "Gross!"

I shrugged again, but this time my shoulders felt strangely heavy.

"I thought Robin was actually kind of cool," said Ali, sounding sad. "That stunt he did at the pool was amazing. And he did help us defeat the big boss at the end of *Revenge of the Robots*."

I spun round to face him. "SO?"

Ali jumped. "Sorry! I was only saying."

"Well, DON'T. I don't want to talk about it, OK?"

"Three out of twenty! That's hilarious!" Jess was feeling smug because she'd got top marks on the test.

"I forgot to learn the stuff," I told her.

It was only Wednesday, but I'd already been told off twice by Mrs Badoe for forgetting to do my homework. Which was why I'd been sitting at the table for the past ten minutes, frowning at a sheet of maths problems. If I didn't get these in on time, I'd be in REAL trouble. Right!

Question one: Savita has three guinea pigs and one cage. How much of the cage does each animal occupy?

"These questions are stupid!" I said, throwing down my pen.

"Are you sure it's the questions that are stupid?" said Jess.

"Ha ha!"

I got up and walked over to give Digby a scratch behind the ears. His tail gave a half-hearted flick, but lacked its usual gusto. The dog hadn't been himself since Mr Burton took Robin away. The robot's hat had found its way into Digby's basket and when Mum had tried to take it off him, Digby had growled and showed his teeth. She'd decided to let him keep it. The hat was covered in dog drool so Mum doubted Dad would want it back now anyway.

A loud sneeze erupted from the front room. Moments later Rosalyn appeared in the doorway and pointed at Digby. "Get that thing out of here! You know the rules."

"If I take him out, will you help me with my homework?" I said.

Our babysitter snorted. "I don't get paid enough to help with homework. Now get rid of that mutt, or I'm telling your mum you've been gaming when you should've been doing schoolwork."

I waited until Rosalyn went back into the other room, then let Digby back in.

"Olivia's been bragging that Mr Burton has got Robin doing all his chores," said Jess.

"I know. Brett says he made Robin cut his toenails!"

My sister made a gagging noise, then shrugged. "Well, he *is* a robot. They're *designed* to do stuff people don't want to do. I mean, it's not like he's a *real* person – with FEELINGS."

I remembered Robin trying to sing while he baked. He'd said it was what people do when they're happy – but robots don't feel emotions. Being Mr Burton's slave couldn't make Robin SAD any more than living with us had made him HAPPY. He was just a machine – a computer on legs!

"That time when Robin asked Mr Rossini to give Digby a shave," said Jess. "*Soooo* embarrassing!"

"Kind of funny too, though," I said. "Remember the way he used to talk to Digby like he was a person?"

My sister snorted. "I thought robots were supposed to be smart!"

"I suppose we all make mistakes."

"Not robots!" said Jess. "That's the whole point! They're designed NOT to make mistakes like humans do."

"Yeah, he wasn't much of a robot really, was he?"

Jess shook her head and opened her

exercise book. I sighed and reached for my pen.

Question two: The mean old man has one robot and ten toenails…

I put the pen down. When I looked up, my sister was staring at me.

"We need to get him back, don't we?" she said.

CHAPTER 10

Operation Rescue Robin

PART 1: BANGING OUR HEADS AGAINST A WALL

Realizing we needed to rescue Robin was the easy part. Working out exactly HOW we were going to do it was much harder.

"Maybe we could break in and steal him back?" I suggested.

Jess raised an eyebrow. "Like prison food, do you?"

"OK, we could BUY him back then. Make Mr Burton an offer he can't refuse!"

"Great idea! How much have you got?"

"Well … not so much at the moment, but

I'm sure Mum owes me some pocket money."

My sister snorted.

"So what ARE we going to do?"

"If you could possibly stop talking for, like, FIVE SECONDS, I might actually be able to think!"

I pulled a face. I was beginning to realize that the hardest part of this whole thing was going to be spending time with Jess. But if we wanted to get Robin back we were going to have to work together.

After a bit more arguing – sorry, *discussion* – we decided to try a TWO-PRONGED ATTACK: I'd talk to Dad while my sister worked on Mum.

"We need to get Robin back from Mr Burton."

"Who?" As usual, Dad was a little slow on the uptake. His driving job meant he was away from home a lot, so he was often a bit behind on current events.

"The robot babysitter Grandma made for us," I reminded him.

Dad frowned. "You mean the maniac who trashed my tomatoes?"

"That was an accident. He … got wet when we went swimming, and it made him go a bit funny."

"A *bit FUNNY*?!" Dad's eyebrows quivered as he gazed at the destruction. "He murdered my tomatoes and obliterated half your mum's paintings!"

"I know, but … he didn't MEAN to."

"I'd been growing those tomatoes for months," Dad said, going all misty-eyed. "I raised them from seed, you know."

It was obvious I wasn't going to get anywhere with him. Maybe Jess would have better luck with Mum.

"She just kept going on about how we could've been hurt," said Jess. "'What if he'd set fire to the house? What if he'd gone crazy with a shovel instead of the hose?' She wouldn't even listen to what I had to say."

"You reminded her about the cakes though, right? How if we got Robin back she could eat delicious muffins every day!"

My sister pulled a face. "Mum said if Robin came back she'd get fat."

I let out a groan of frustration. "What is WRONG with these people?"

"We'll just have to think of a way to get him back ourselves," said Jess. "Any ideas?"

Sometimes the best way to find a solution to a problem is *not* to go looking for one. You can be banging your head against a brick wall, trying SO HARD to think of something, and get nowhere. But if you *stop* trying – if you forget about it for a while and do something else – a strange and magical thing can happen, and the answer just pops up all by itself!

I decided to play some *Revenge of the Robots* to clear my head. While I was playing, I remembered what Robin had said about being ashamed of the robots in the game and how they'd misbehaved…

And that's when I had my genius idea.

"You want to get Robin to trash Mr Burton's house like he did our garden?" I couldn't tell if Jess was impressed or about to start laughing.

"If we can make Mr Burton think that Robin *is* really dangerous," I said. "Well … he won't *want* to keep him then, will he?"

Jess frowned. "That's actually not such a bad idea…"

"It's genius!"

My sister snorted. "OK then, Einstein, so how are we going to get Robin to deliberately malfunction again? We can't exactly go next door and ask if we can give him a bath!"

"Um … I haven't worked that bit out yet."

Jess rolled her eyes.

"What? I'm supposed to think of EVERYTHING now, am I?"

I put Grandma on speaker so Jess could hear too.

"First you let Donald Burton steal my lovely robot and now you want to make him DELIBERATELY malfunction!"

I was glad Grandma was on the phone and not within swiping range. I also wondered how she knew Mr Burton's name was Donald, but now probably wasn't the time to ask. She was NOT using her happy voice.

"I programmed layers of safety code to make sure something like that DIDN'T happen," she said.

"So it can't be done?"

"Now I didn't say *that*, did I?" Grandma's voice softened a little. "Let me have a cup of tea and a think. I reckon it could be a THREE-CUP PROBLEM, this, so you'd better give me at least an hour."

Three cups of tea and half a packet of Jammie Dodgers later...

"It goes against the fundamental Laws of Robotics for a robot to act against its owner," said Grandma, still crunching on the remains of a biscuit, "but there is a way *you* could control him remotely."

I grinned at Jess. "How?"

"I programmed a fail-safe to allow remote access in an emergency," said Grandma. "It's paired with your games console, so in theory you could control him from there. It would be just like playing a game."

"Brilliant! So what do we do? What are the controls?"

"One step at a time!" said Grandma. "First you have to ACTIVATE remote access."

"OK, so how do we do that?"

"You have to sing to him."

"Pardon?!" said Jess. "I think the phone went funny just then, Grandma. It sounded like you said we have to SING to the robot."

"That's right." We could hear Grandma chuckling to herself. "I told you it was an EMERGENCY measure. I didn't think you'd ever have to use it! I programmed Robin's fail-safe to respond to your voices, but it couldn't just be your normal *speaking* voices or you could have set it off accidentally. I used that recording you sent for my birthday – the two of you singing 'Happy Birthday' to me."

"So we have to sing 'Happy Birthday' to the

robot?" I said. That recording had been Mum's idea. A painful half an hour of my life that I was in no hurry to revisit. "There must be another way!"

"I'm afraid not. If you want to take control, you're going to have to sing to him."

Suddenly the plan seemed a lot less brilliant.

CHAPTER 11

Operation Rescue Robin

PART 2: TWO LOSERS AND A DOG SING 'HAPPY BIRTHDAY'!

It's kind of disappointing how ideas that seemed GREAT at the planning stage suddenly feel COMPLETELY LUDICROUS on a chilly Friday evening when you're walking next door to sing 'Happy Birthday' in front of your neighbour's house!

Part of me hoped that Rosalyn would demand to know what we were doing and stop us from going out, but she didn't even notice us leave.

I started to wonder if we really needed to

rescue Robin. I mean, hadn't we WANTED to get rid of him? I remembered all the times he'd embarrassed us and how Robin wouldn't let us do anything until our homework was finished; how he'd always know if we tried to fake being ill. On the other hand, he *had* helped me and Ali defeat the big boss in *Revenge of the Robots* and, unlike Rosalyn, Robin actually seemed to like spending time with us.

Then I started thinking about Robin trying to sing when we were baking. Robots weren't supposed to *feel* emotions, but maybe Robin was different ... special?

We had to rescue him. He was *our* robot! No! More than that – he was our FRIEND.

There was no way we could abandon him to Mr Burton, even if getting him back did mean totally embarrassing ourselves in public – again!

At least it was nearly dark. Hopefully there'd

be nobody around to see us make fools of ourselves this time.

So there we were, standing on Mr Burton's doorstep, singing 'Happy Birthday' like a pair of really confused carol singers. Jess was really going for it – belting out the song like it was the final of *Britain's Got Talent*.

Now I'll admit that sometimes I'm not as kind to my twin as I could be but, when I tell you that Jess can NOT sing, I'm not being horrible because she's my sister – it's simply the truth. If your ears were unfortunate enough to hear my sister sing, they would tell you exactly the same thing.

I was doing my best to join in because Grandma said that Robin was programmed to respond to *both* our voices. Digby was there too, doing what he always does when Jess sings: throwing his head back and HOWLING! (I don't know if he's complaining or joining in. Dogs have strange taste in music…)

The noise we were making was quite … something. Thankfully 'Happy Birthday' is a short song, so we got to the end pretty quickly. Then we looked at each other, not sure what was supposed to happen next.

Usually this was the point where someone blows out the candles and everyone gets a slice of cake. Of course on this occasion there was no cake. What we wanted was some kind of sign that Robin had heard us. But the house was silent.

"Maybe we should sing it again?" said Jess.

So we did.

Again.

And again.

And again.

And—

Mr Burton's front door flew open and the old man shot out like the house was on fire.

"WHAT DO YOU THINK YOU'RE DOING?" he shouted, flapping his arms at us. **"STOP THAT INFERNAL RACKET THIS INSTANT!"**

Believe me, I wanted to stop, but with the door open this was our best chance of getting Robin to hear us. So we kept singing.

I saw movement in the hallway behind Mr Burton and for a moment I thought it was the robot. Then I realized that the shape filling the doorway was too short and too wide … and it was pointing a mobile phone at us.

"This is going straight on YouTube," said Brett, laughing so hard he was struggling to hold the camera still. "*Two Losers and a Dog Sing 'Happy Birthday'!* Viral for sure."

Of course we had to choose an evening when Brett was visiting.

We reached the end of the song and this
time we did stop.

"Mum said it was your birthday," said Jess,
giving Mr Burton her best innocent smile. "So
we thought it would be nice if we came round
to sing to you."

For a few seconds the old man was so taken
aback he just stared at us. Then he scowled.

"Your mother is mistaken," he said. "It's
NOT my birthday, so you can go away."

Then his eyes narrowed and he leaned closer. "I know what you're up to," he hissed. "But it won't work. You're not getting it back."

"I don't know what you're talking about," I said, trying not to shiver.

Brett was still laughing as we walked away. "Weirdos!" he shouted.

"That better have worked," said Jess.

I nodded. If Robin hadn't heard our singing, all we'd done was give Brett a new video to humiliate us with.

CHAPTER 12

Operation Rescue Robin

PART 3: BAD ROBOT

I'd never felt so nervous waiting for my console to start up. Jess was sitting next to me on the bed with Digby – he could sense there was something important going on and didn't want to miss out.

"What are we going to do if it didn't work?" Jess asked.

"Run away to a country where they don't have YouTube?" I suggested, entering my login details.

The row of game icons slid into view and

there it was – Robin's face, all bushy beard and wonky football hat.

"It worked!" said Jess. "I told you my singing was the best!"

Normally I would have had something to say about that, but I'd just remembered that Grandma never got around to telling me HOW I was supposed to control the robot once we got access!

I selected the icon and a message flashed up on the screen.

ROBOT REMOTE CONTROL INITIATED.

SELECT 'Y' TO PROCEED. 'N' TO EXIT.

I glanced at Jess and Digby. "Are we sure about this?"

Digby gave a low woof and slapped his tail against the bed. My sister nodded. "Let's get our robot back!"

I clicked the button and the television filled with the image of a kitchen. There was the cooker and a sink… The picture was moving, as though the person holding the camera was in motion. The view descended until a washing machine filled the screen, and for a second we saw a face reflected in the circular glass door.

Digby sat up and barked, his tail whipping the air like a helicopter.

"It's Robin!" said Jess.

"We must be getting a live feed from the robot's eyes," I said. "We get to see what he sees!"

A hand wearing a yellow rubber glove opened the washer and started pulling clothes into a basket on the floor.

"Ugh!" said Jess. "Are those…?"

I nodded. "Looks like Mr Burton's got Robin doing his washing. We REALLY need to get him out of there."

"So go on then. You've got control. Only maybe try not to get killed as many times as you usually do."

"WHAT D'YOU MEAN?" But I knew EXACTLY what she meant.

When I start a new game, I'm always rubbish until I get used to it. And this time there was no tutorial, no chance to practise. This time, if anyone got hurt … it would be FOR REAL.

For a second I just sat there, staring at the screen, the controller all sweaty in my hands.

Then I told myself to get a grip. I could do this. I just needed to pretend I was playing *Revenge of the Robots*, only this time we wanted the robot to win!

So . . . in *Revenge* the right-hand joystick lets you look around. Maybe that would work here.

"Oh, my!" said Robin's voice as the view on the television swung to the right.

"Of course!" I said. "He doesn't know he's

being controlled! Robin must think his head just moved all on its own!"

Robin put Mr Burton's underwear in the drier then the view changed to a pile of dirty dishes next to the sink. The yellow rubber gloves squirted some liquid into the washing-up bowl, then turned on the taps.

"Right," I muttered. "Let's see what this baby can do!"

I nudged the controller and Robin started walking towards the door.

"What's happening to me?" he said. "My legs – they're moving on their own! Stop it! Naughty legs!"

I felt bad for freaking him out, but we had no way to let Robin know what we were doing.

I could see the front door at the end of the hallway, and so far there was no sign of Mr Burton. Maybe I could get Robin to simply open the door and walk home.

But if we did that Mr Burton would just come round and demand him back. We needed Robin to trash the place and scare the life out of the old man – make him think Robin really *was* dangerous. Plus our neighbour deserved to be taught a lesson for treating Robin like a slave. It was time for this robot to take HIS revenge!

"Hey!" said Jess, grabbing my arm. "Can you hear that?"

There was music coming from the room on Robin's left.

"That's from *Beauty and the Beast!*" said Jess.

"I never had Mr Burton down as a *Beauty*

and the Beast fan," I said, guiding Robin through the doorway.

But it wasn't Mr Burton dancing round, singing 'Tale as Old as Time' in front of the giant TV mounted on the wall…

Brett jumped, his race flushing red. "What do YOU want, robot?"

Of course Brett couldn't see us – he thought it was just Robin he was talking to.

"Get me a drink," he said, "and a muffin. No, make that two!" Brett looked down at the doll in the yellow dress

he was clutching. "You want one, too, don't you, Belle?"

"No way!"
I whispered. "Is he pretending to be Beast?"

"If people at

school knew about this," said Jess, "he'd never be able to bully anyone ever again!"

"Funny you should say that." I pointed to the flashing red dot in the corner of the screen.

"What's that?"

"I'm recording all of this. I could upload to YouTube straight from here!"

Her eyes widened. "We can't! Can we?"

"We *could* – and that's all that matters! Once Brett knows we've got this…" I grinned.

"What are you waiting for?" shouted Brett. "A Coke and two muffins. NOW!"

"Very good, Master Brett," said the robot.

Robin had just walked back into the hall when a roar of anger erupted from the kitchen.

"Looks like we've found Mr Burton," I said.

"And he's found out Robin left the taps running," said Jess. "Oops!"

We watched Mr Burton splash across the kitchen to the sink, then turn to face Robin.

"WHAT DO YOU THINK YOU'RE DOING, ROBOT?"

"I'm terribly sorry, sir," said Robin. "I don't know what's happening to me. I think I might have a bug in my system."

Mr Burton's ratty face filled the screen. "Wouldn't surprise me," he muttered. "Shoddy programming. I'll have to open you up and investigate. But first you can clean up this mess. And when you've done that there are leaves all over the drive." He pointed to the motorized leaf-blower lying on the table next to a plate of freshly baked muffins.

Robin shook his head. Or rather I wobbled the joystick so his head swung from left to right, but to Mr Burton it looked like the robot was shaking his head.

"WHAT?" Mr Burton's eyes bulged. "Did you just shake your head at me, robot?"

"NO, sir!" said Robin, nodding his head. "I'm

sorry, sir. I don't know what's the matter with me. I seem to have lost control of my body. Maybe I should try a reboot."

Robin's gloved hand loomed towards the screen.

"Quick!" said Jess. "DO SOMETHING! Before he shuts himself down!"

"I DON'T KNOW WHAT THE CONTROLS ARE!"

"Oh, give it to me!" My sister grabbed the controller and stabbed at the buttons. The robot started waving his arms around.

"What on earth—?" Mr Burton took a step back.

Jess pressed another button and Robin picked up a muffin from the plate on the table.

"*Now* what are you doing?" said Mr Burton.

"I appear to have picked up a muffin, sir. Ah, that's right! Master Brett requested some refreshments."

"I wonder…" I said.

"What?" Jess looked at me.

"Try the FIRE button!"

The muffin flew over Mr Burton's head and exploded against the wall.

"Like that?" said Jess.

"Yeah, except you're aiming at him, not the wall!"

"GIVE ME A CHANCE!" Jess leaned forwards, her tongue poking out from the side of her mouth. "So circle to pick stuff up, then aim and…"

If the old man hadn't ducked, the second muffin would definitely have hit him.

"Sir! I'm so sorry! I don't know what's come over me," said Robin. "BAD ROBOT!"

"What's going on?" said Brett's voice. "Where're my muffins?"

"You want muffins?" said Jess, spinning Robin round. "I'll give you muffins!"

Brett was so shocked he didn't move until the first cake hit him in the face.

"Tell me we're still recording!" said Jess as Brett turned and ran screaming back down the hall, chunks of double-choc muffin falling from his hair.

We were having so much fun I'd almost forgotten about Mr Burton until I saw his hands appear and start fumbling for the reset button up the robot's nose.

"NO! DON'T LET HIM RESET OR WE'LL LOSE CONTROL!"

"AGGHH!" said Jess, frantically pressing buttons. "I CAN'T GET HIM OFF!"

I grabbed back the controller and spun Robin round. Mr Burton swore as the move shook him off on to the soggy floor. The old man got up, dripping wet and purple with rage.

There were no more muffins left, just the leaf-blower on the table. I made Robin pick it up.

"Oh, no!" said the robot.

"Oh, yes!" said Jess.

Rosalyn nearly dropped her phone when Robin came crashing through the front door, wielding a leaf-blower. Then she was off the sofa and out of the house before you could say, 'I'm not getting paid enough for THIS!'

My sister couldn't stop grinning. "You'd have thought Robin had a chainsaw, not a leaf-blower the way he scared them off!" Brett and Mr Burton had also run screaming down the road.

"Who knew they were so powerful?" I said. "I didn't think it would make quite that much mess!"

"Serves him right," said Jess. "He shouldn't have stolen our robot and used him as a slave."

"You think Robin will be all right?"

The robot was sitting in his chair next to Digby's bed. He'd arrived in such a state we had to shut him down. The dog was lying at Robin's feet, licking muffin crumbs off the roller skates and thumping his tail against the kitchen lino.

"He'll be fine," said Jess. "He's home now. We did it!"

We grinned and high-fived, then suddenly realized what we were doing and jumped apart.

"Mum's not going to be happy when she sees he's back," said Jess.

I nodded. Why was it that just when you thought you'd solved one problem, there always seemed to be another waiting to jump out at you?

LESS ROBOT, MORE HUMAN!

The school fair started at noon. All morning
the house had been filled with the mouth-
watering aroma of freshly baked muffins.

"Are we all ready?" said Mum for the tenth
time. "You've got the cakes?"

"Yes, ma'am. The muffins are secured and
ready for transportation," said Robin.

"What's left of them," muttered Jess.

Mum blushed. "I just wanted to make sure
they were all right before we unleashed them
on the public!"

"You look very smart today, Robin," said Dad, who had the weekend off for a change. "I like your suit. In fact I've got one just like it."

Me and Jess exchanged a look.

"We didn't think Grandma's coat really suited him," said Jess.

"He looks like Batman's butler now," I said.

"Except Alfred doesn't have a beard … or curly hair!" Jess pointed out.

As well as *borrowing* Dad's suit, we'd found a wig in a charity shop. It didn't quite fit the look I was going for, but it was better than a dog-chewed woolly hat. Jess had painted the Barbie skates black so they looked more like shoes too.

It was quite a makeover, but it had all helped to persuade Mum and Dad to let Robin stay.

It hadn't been easy. Mum had actually screamed when she saw the robot had returned. Luckily Grandma was back from InventorCon and came round straight away when we phoned. She gave Robin what she called a "full medical and software update".

"He's perfectly safe now," she told Mum, giving us a wink. "I switched him off and on again!" she whispered. "If he has another funny turn, you know what to do…" Grandma raised a finger and jabbed it upwards.

The robot was no longer linked to my console, but Grandma had reprogrammed remote access to activate from a special code we could send Robin via Wi-Fi, should we need to take control in future.

Mr Burton had no idea we'd been involved in Robin's 'malfunction', but he still came round to complain about the damage 'our' robot had done to his house.

Grandma answered the door. We didn't hear what she said to him, but the old man didn't stay long. When I asked her how she knew Mr Burton's name was Donald, Grandma looked strangely shifty and said it was, "A long story … for another time." She refused to say more, no matter how much me and Jess begged.

It took most of the week and multiple batches of muffins to convince Mum to give Robin another chance. The fact that Rosalyn phoned to say she was never coming back, no matter how much Mum paid her, probably helped too.

The school hall was already busy when we arrived. There were tables set out along the walls and down the middle, selling everything from cakes and plastic beakers of warm, spicy apple punch to Halloween decorations and Christmas cards.

Robin delivered his tins to the cake stall. Ten minutes later word had spread about the apple-and-cinnamon muffins and there was a queue stretching out of the door.

We met up with Ivana and Ali, and at the end of the first row of stalls we bumped into Mrs Badoe.

"Oh, I am sorry!" she said. "I forget there's a lot more of me these days!"

"When's the baby due, miss?" Ivana asked.

"Just after Christmas, so you'll be getting a new teacher next term."

Ivana and Jess groaned, which made Mrs Badoe smile, but she was anxious to move on. "I heard about some amazing apple-and-cinnamon muffins," she said. "I'm hoping they haven't all gone!"

"I wonder who our new teacher will be?" said Jess as Mrs Badoe hurried away. "Whoever it is won't be as nice as her."

"Hey, why don't we go and have a look over there?" said Ali, changing direction so suddenly I almost walked into him. Then I saw why.

Olivia, Brett and Drool were gathered round a Halloween stall up ahead – we would have blundered straight into them.

Brett saw us and nudged Olivia.

"Uh-oh!" said Ivana.

But then a strange thing happened. Rather than homing in on us, they turned and fled in the opposite direction. If you didn't know better, you'd have thought THEY were scared of US!

"What's with them?" said Ali.

"Maybe Brett's decided he should stop being such a BEAST to everyone!" said Jess. We both burst out laughing until we realized

Ali and Ivana were staring blankly at us. They knew nothing about the video we had of Brett. But *he* did and that was what mattered.

We'd cornered Brett earlier in the week and shown him the clip. He'd looked so shocked and confused I'd felt sorry for him, until I remembered all the times he'd picked on Ali and everyone else. We'd promised not to tell anybody about his *Beauty and the Beast* moment if he stopped hassling people at school.

So far it seemed to be working.

It was time for Jess to go in goal on the penalty shoot-out stall (Mrs Badoe had let her and Liesha share goalkeeping duties), so we followed her outside.

There was a row of games at the edge of the field, offering high-octane thrills like Guess the Number of Smarties in the Jar, and Bash the Rat! (The stallholder dropped a knitted grey rat down a piece of old drainpipe and you had to try to whack it with a plastic rounders bat when it fell out at the bottom.) They were the kind of games that got Dad all nostalgic. His absolute favourite was the Coconut Shy. It was also his nemesis. Every year Dad tried, and failed, to knock one of the coconuts off and win a prize.

Unlike Dad, it turned out that Robin was really good at all the games – and I mean

REALLY good. After he'd guessed the number of Smarties in the Jar EXACTLY and Bashed the Rat so hard it almost went into orbit, we had to tell him to take it easy in case people got suspicious.

"You mean I should fail deliberately?" said Robin. "Like your father does?"

"Just be a little less robot and a bit more human," I told him.

"Yeah — be rubbish like the rest of us!" said Ali, laughing.

Dad was still trying his luck with the Coconut Shy and as usual failing miserably. On the rare occasion he actually hit one of the coconuts, it still didn't fall off.

Robin watched for a while, then when Dad's turn was over asked if he could have a go.

I wasn't sure that was such a good idea. Dad wouldn't be happy if Robin knocked all the coconuts off with his first attempt! I didn't want to give him and Mum any reason to change their minds about keeping the robot. But Robin was already lining up his first throw.

"Remember – *less robot, more human!*" I whispered in his ear.

"Very well, Master Just Jake," said Robin and hurled the ball at the line of coconuts.

It struck the target, but the fruit didn't fall. I winced.

"Nice shot!" said the stallholder.

Robin threw again. This time he hit the coconut in the middle. Again the ball bounced off.

"Unlucky!" said the man. "Just not quite enough power!"

Dad frowned.

"ROBIN!" I hissed, but the robot didn't seem to hear.

When his final throw cannoned into the last coconut in the line, the wooden ball actually

split in two,
but the coconut
still didn't budge.

"I think you
could say
that one
was hard
enough!"
said Mum.

"There's
something
going on here!"

Dad strode up to the line of coconuts and
tried to lift one off its stand. "Ha! Just as I
suspected! They're glued on!"

The stallholder tried to move Dad away,

but Robin clamped his shoulder
with a robotic hand. "I think you
owe this gentleman an apology,"
he said. "And a prize!"

"All these years," said Dad, clutching an armful of coconuts. "I thought it was ME!" He shook his head. "You just can't trust some people!"

"You know robots are programmed to always tell the truth," I said. "Robin, for example – he wouldn't be allowed to lie even if he wanted to."

"Is that right?" said Dad. "I'm impressed the way he saw what that bloke was up to."

"Robin's very good at spotting fakes," said Jess, back from her shift in goal. "It's been quite useful actually."

"I wish I had a robot for a babysitter," said Ivana.

"Yeah, you two are well lucky!" said Ali. "Robin's AWESOME."

Me and Jess exchanged a look.

We didn't say anything, but I could tell

my sister was thinking the same as me: Ali and Ivana were right – having a robot for a babysitter WAS kind of awesome.

"Um, Jake?" Ali tugged my sleeve and pointed to where Robin was juggling coconuts for an admiring crowd of onlookers. "Those coconuts he's juggling. They're not ALL coconuts!"

The dog was fine, though he did keep walking in circles for a while afterwards. But, to be fair to Robin, Digby is small, round and hairy – it was an easy mistake to make.

The End (… for now!)

TURN THE PAGE FOR
A SNEAK PEEK AT
THE NEXT STORY IN
THE SERIES...

IS MY TEACHER A ROBOT?

CHAPTER 1

ON THE LAST DAY
OF CHRISTMAS

"A ROBOT?" Dad snorted at the TV. "That's just a vacuum cleaner with a face painted on it!"

We were watching the *Buy It or Bin It?* Christmas special. People go on the show and present an invention to a panel of investors. The panel then decides if the idea is worth an investment and buy it, or reject it to the bin! Mum and Dad were hooked.

"Fleur looks quite interested," said Mum, as the camera zoomed in on one of the judges.

"She used to live round here, you know?"
said Dad.

"You say that every time," I told him, rolling
my eyes.

Dad shrugged. "She's worth billions!"

The woman on the telly was called Fleur
Pickles. She was probably about the same
age as Dad, but she looked … less worn,
somehow. Being a billionaire probably helped.
It was good to know that somebody from a
nowhere town like ours could get rich and
even end up on TV.

"We should get Grandma to go on this,"
said Dad. "The stuff she invents is way
better!"

Mum nearly spat out her chocolate.
"Are you serious? Have you forgotten what
happened when Digby got too close to that
AUTOMATIC TURKEY STUFFER she made?
The poor dog hasn't been the same since!"

She shuddered. "And as for that **SNOW MACHINE** … we're lucky it was only *our* windows that got broken. Those hailstones were the size of golf balls!"

"Yeah, but think of the money she'd make if she sold one of her ideas," said Dad. "Where *is* Digby, anyway?"

"With Robin, I expect."

Robin is probably Grandma's most successful invention. She built him to look after me and Jess while Mum and Dad were at work. He looks so much like a real person, most people don't even realize he's a robot.

The judges on *Buy It or Bin It?* were about to announce their decision when we heard an ominous crash from the direction of the kitchen.

"I'll go!" I said quickly. Mum and Dad quite like having a robot around, but Robin has a habit of getting into trouble. They got rid of him once before – I didn't want them to have a reason to do it again.

I made sure to close the door behind me.

"Is that YOU making all that noise?" My sister was standing at the bottom of the stairs, scowling. It's her favourite facial expression. "Have you seen Digby?"

"I think he's in there … with Robin." I nodded towards the kitchen.

"So what are you waiting for?" Jess is always telling me what to do – like she's my *big* sister – when in fact we're twins, so exactly the same age.

"Why don't *you* go in?" I said.

"You're closest!"

I sighed and opened the door.

The kitchen was unrecognizable. It felt as though you were walking into a jungle made from Christmas paper, dangling like multi-coloured vines from the ceiling.

I was barely over the threshold when something lurched at me from the undergrowth. It was like a giant spider, all spindly limbs and quick, jerky movements. One of its arms ended with a pair of shining blades that snipped the air in front of my face.

I ducked, narrowly avoiding an unscheduled haircut, then stumbled into a transparent web of sticky tape.

The creature pounced.

In seconds I was wrapped in a Christmas cocoon, unable to move.

"Robin!" I shouted. "It's ME!"

"Master Just Jake! Oh, my!" The robot apologized and started to cut me free. "You stepped into my production line. I thought you were a gift that needed wrapping!"

"You do know Christmas is over, right?" said Jess.

"But your mother was disappointed when

your grandma's **RAPID-WRAP-IT!** machine didn't work," said the robot. "I thought I would see if I could improve on it."

"I don't think Mum wanted you to gift wrap the kitchen though," I said.

Robin stroked his beard, a sign he was thinking. "My procedure is still in the development stage. I repeat a task and refine the process until it runs smoothly."

"It's a good job you've got a whole year until next Christmas," said Jess. "I'd say *this* process needs a *lot* of refining!"

I looked around at the web of tape stretching across the kitchen, bits of wrapping caught up in it like festive flies. "By the way, have you seen Digby? I thought he was with you."

"Digby? He's just…" Robin turned towards the pile of presents. "Oh, dear!"

We'd rescued Digby and were trying to *unwrap* the kitchen when the doorbell rang.

Dad's footsteps thumped along the hall, then we heard our neighbour's voice.

Mr Burton reminds me of a vampire. He has a pointy nose and grey bushy eyebrows like two hairy caterpillars clinging to his forehead.

We watched through a crack in the door as he handed Dad a note. "It's a bill," he said. "For the damage your robot caused to my house when it malfunctioned."

Me and Jess exchanged a look. We knew a lot more about Robin's *malfunction* than anybody realized – but that's another story.

"This seems expensive!" said Dad.

"Removing chocolate muffin from a cream carpet is not easy," said Mr Burton. "Besides, there was the leaf-blower." He shuddered.

Even I'd been surprised how powerful *that* had turned out to be.

"I must go and apologize," said Robin. "Your father should not have to pay for damage I caused."

"NO! Don't go out there!" I put my body between Robin and the door. "It's better if Mr Burton doesn't know you're still here."

Meanwhile, Dad and the old man were still talking.

"There may be an alternative solution," said Mr Burton. "If the robot was to come and work for me, he could repair the damage himself – at no cost to you."

"That proposal is a very logical solution," said Robin. "I wish to accept."

"NO!" said Jess. "Have you forgotten what happened last time?"

"Mr Burton treated you like a slave!" I reminded him. "He made you cut his toenails!"

But the robot wasn't listening. He made another lunge towards the door, so Jess jumped on his back while Digby took hold of a trouser leg in his teeth. But Robin is surprisingly strong, and even the three of us together couldn't stop him.

Dad looked surprised when the kitchen door flew open and Robin burst into the hallway with me, Jess, and Digby still clinging on.

"I wondered where you lot were," he said.

"Where's Mr Burton?" said Jess.

"He left." Dad raised an eyebrow. "I'm guessing you were listening?"

"You're not going to make Robin go and work for him are you?" I said.

"I told him I needed to talk it over with your mum."

"It is right that I should repair the damage I caused," said Robin.

"Well … hopefully it won't come to that." Dad smiled. "Now, I don't suppose there are any mince pies left are there?" He moved towards the kitchen but Jess jumped in the way.

"I'll get you one! Why don't you go and sit down? You don't want to miss the end of *Buy It or Bin It?* do you."

Dad nodded. "Good point! Thanks, love!"

"That was close," said Jess when he'd gone. "Jake, you help Robin clear up this mess while I keep Mum and Dad distracted with mince pies."

Normally I would have argued, but I was too busy thinking that Mr Burton would be back, and it was going to take a lot more than mince pies to keep *him* distracted.

ABOUT THE AUTHOR

Abandoning childhood plans to be an astronaut –
or Batman – Dave Cousins went to art college in
Bradford, joined a band and was nearly famous.
His writing career began aged ten, drawing comics
and penning lyrics for an imaginary pop group.
Dave says that reading and writing stories helped him
along the bumpy path to growing-up, and hopes that his
books will play a similar role for today's readers.

When not scribbling stories and pictures,
Dave tours extensively. His events have been
described as "stand-up with books", or as
one reader put it: "well funny!" Dave has three
grown-up children and lives on a rock by the sea
in Wales, with his wife and a grumpy cat.

www.davecousins.net

ABOUT THE ILLUSTRATOR

Born in Bogotá, Colombia,
Catalina Echeverri lives in London with her
Northern Irish husband, Will and their little daughter S.

Before settling in the UK Catalina spent time in Italy,
studying graphic design and eating pizza and ice cream
every day that she could. When she'd eaten it all, she
moved to Cambridge to study children's book illustration.
She has worked in children's publishing ever since, creating
books such as *Milo's Dog Says Moo,*
There's a Dinosaur in my Bathtub and *Lion and Mouse.*

Catalina is never without her sketchbook.
She particularly enjoys working on projects that
make a positive impact on people's lives.

www.cataverri.com

ACKNOWLEDGEMENTS

Writing a story is a solitary task, but turning
that story into a book requires a whole team of
people. I would like to thank everyone involved in
producing the book you are holding.

To Ruth and the fantastic team at Stripes
and Little Tiger, thanks for inviting me to write a
story about a robot babysitter – especially Rachel
Boden, who had the idea to create a robot to
babysit the twins, and to Mattie for helping me get
the resulting chaos down on paper! Rachel – we
hope you're happy with the way it turned out!

For me, stories are all about the characters,
so special thanks to Cata for bringing the people
in this story to life with her wonderful illustrations.
Respect and gratitude to Pip and her team for
turning our collection of words and pictures into a
proper book!

To my agent Jenny Savill, appreciation for her continued support and encouragement, and for getting me the gig! Love and thanks to my family for putting up with me and my random, and often bizarre questions, such as: "what do you think a robot would do if...?" Extra thanks to Dylan for the gaming advice!

Finally, a special mention for all the librarians, teachers, booksellers and parents out there – thanks for all the work you do bringing books to readers – without a reader, a story is just words on a page. So thank YOU for reading this book. I hope you enjoy it and many more in the future. Hey – why not try writing or drawing one of your own? We ALL have a story to tell...

Dave Cousins, March 2019

THE ADVENTURES
WILL CONTINUE IN...

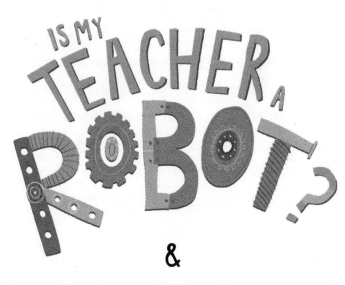

IS MY TEACHER A ROBOT?

&

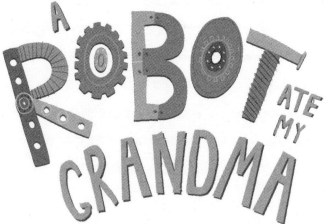

A ROBOT ATE MY GRANDMA

COMING SOON!